For Avila, Brynn, Nathaniel, Ashton, and everyone who has ever let one rip - Ashley

For my sister, Ashley, my daughters, Beatrix, Kit and Ginger, and all girls of today and tomorrow - Arwen

For my children, Cole and Annabel - Sandie

2019 Santa Cruz, California

ISBN Numbers: 978-1-7331374-0-9 (soft cover) & 978-1-7331374-1-6 (hardcover)

Library of Congress Control Number: 2019907338

We Toot!

Written by
Ashley Wheelock
&
Arwen Evans

Illustrated by
Sandie Sonke

House of Tomorrow

What smells like a skunk and sounds like a frog? What trumpets and hoots, and barks like a dog?

Bark! Ribbit!

What wafts in the room, overpowers
the nose? I'll tell you quite plainly, it
isn't a rose.

My friend had a party, the slumbering kind. We all brought our bags, began to unwind.

Ate candy and pizza, played movies and games.

Told silly stories, made outlandish claims.

Then we were sleepy, curled up nice and tight. Snuggled with stuffies, to sleep through the night.

When morning came, the fun started anew. With dancing and laughing, when out of the blue:

There was a loud sound,
that went

brroommm
broommm
bbrroom

All paused to listen...

They all stared at me.
Oh, what should I do?

Then in came our friend,
she looked all around.

What is the
problem?

She started laughing, put her hand on her heart.

I swear it was me, I fart all the time. I'm not ashamed of this body of mine.

You can't tell me you don't, because all of us do. It's totally natural, you know that is true.

She smiled slightly, and just then I knew. I had to back her...

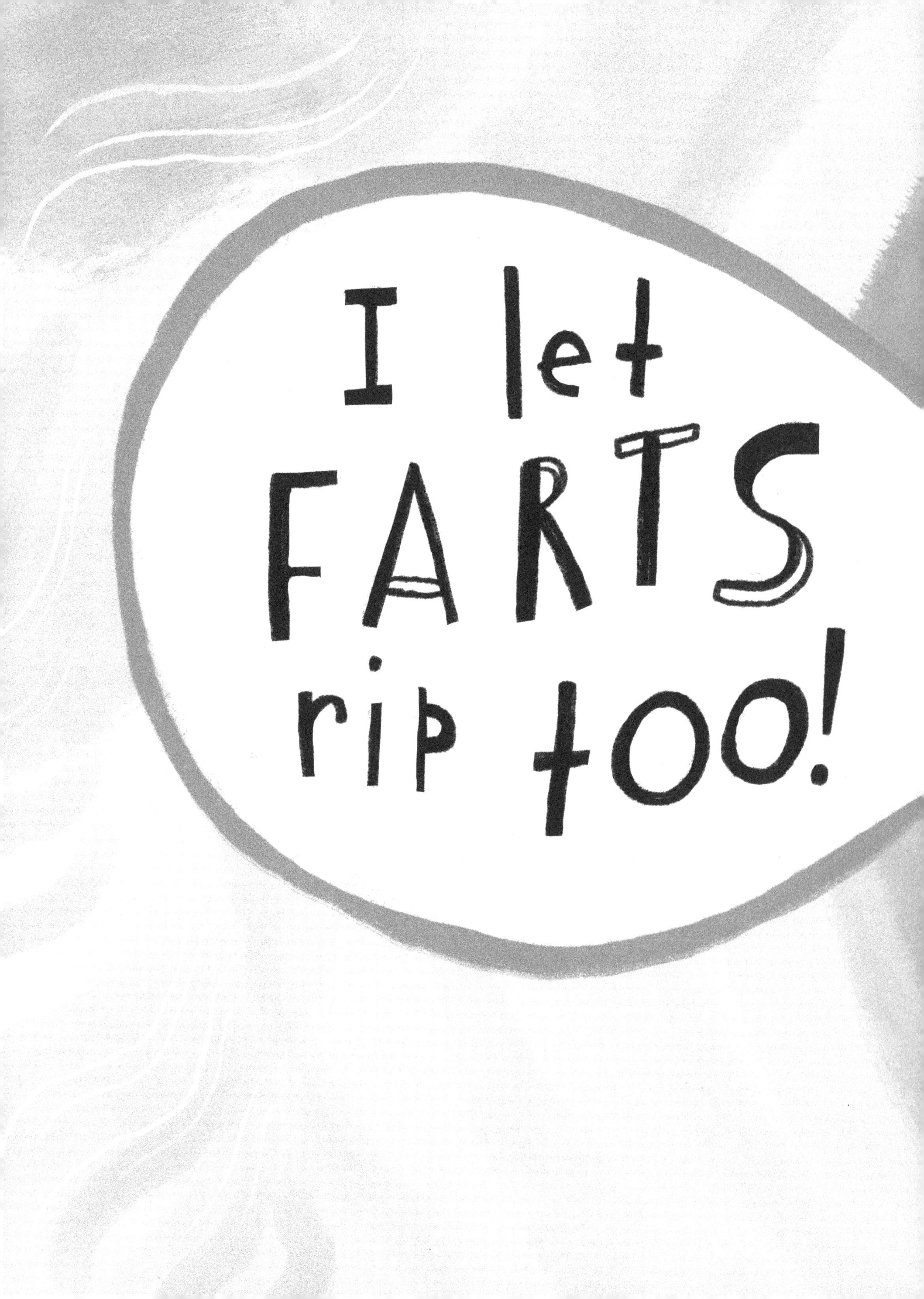
I let FARTS rip too!

Said another.

Me too.

Said a third.

Me toot!

Said a fourth.

Then the last girl concurred.

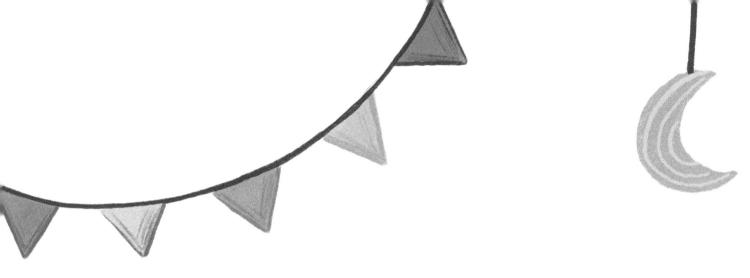

We started to giggle, then chuckle, then snort.

HA! HA! HA! giggle

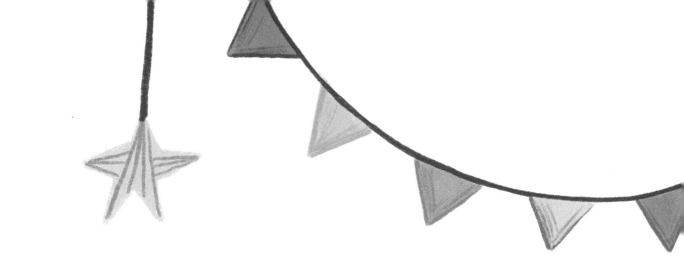

We all had each other, we all had support.

giggle   Hee Hee Hee
snort   HA! HA!

Our bodies are wonders, each with its own quirks.

You can't have another.
They're all masterworks.

So appreciate it for all that it does.
And just love yourself, simply because.

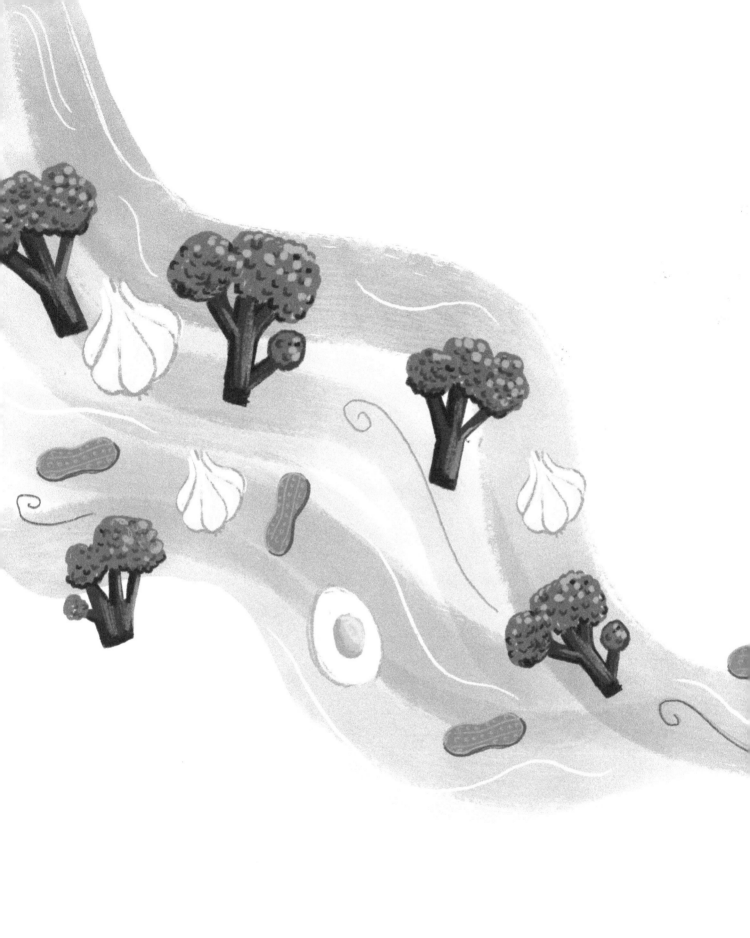

CPSIA information can be obtained
at www.ICGtesting.com
Printed in the USA
LVHW070736180220
647294LV00020B/158